ANTHONY BROWNE

The Little Bear Book

CANDLEWICK PRESS

First Candlewick Press edition 2014

First published by Hamish Hamilton Children's Books

Library of Congress Catalog Card Number 2013944021
ISBN 978-0-7636-7007-8

14 15 16 17 18 19 TLF 10 9 8 7 6 5 4 3 2 1

Printed in Dongguan, Guangdong, China

This book was typeset in New Century Schoolbook.
The illustrations were done in watercolor and ink.

Candlewick Press
99 Dover Street
Somerville, Massachusetts 02144

visit us at www.candlewick.com

Bear went for a walk.

"Hello, Gorilla."

“I know what you need.”

“Hello, Crocodile.”

“This will keep you quiet.”

"Hello, Lion."

"Here's just the thing for you."

“What’s this?”

“Hello, Elephant.”

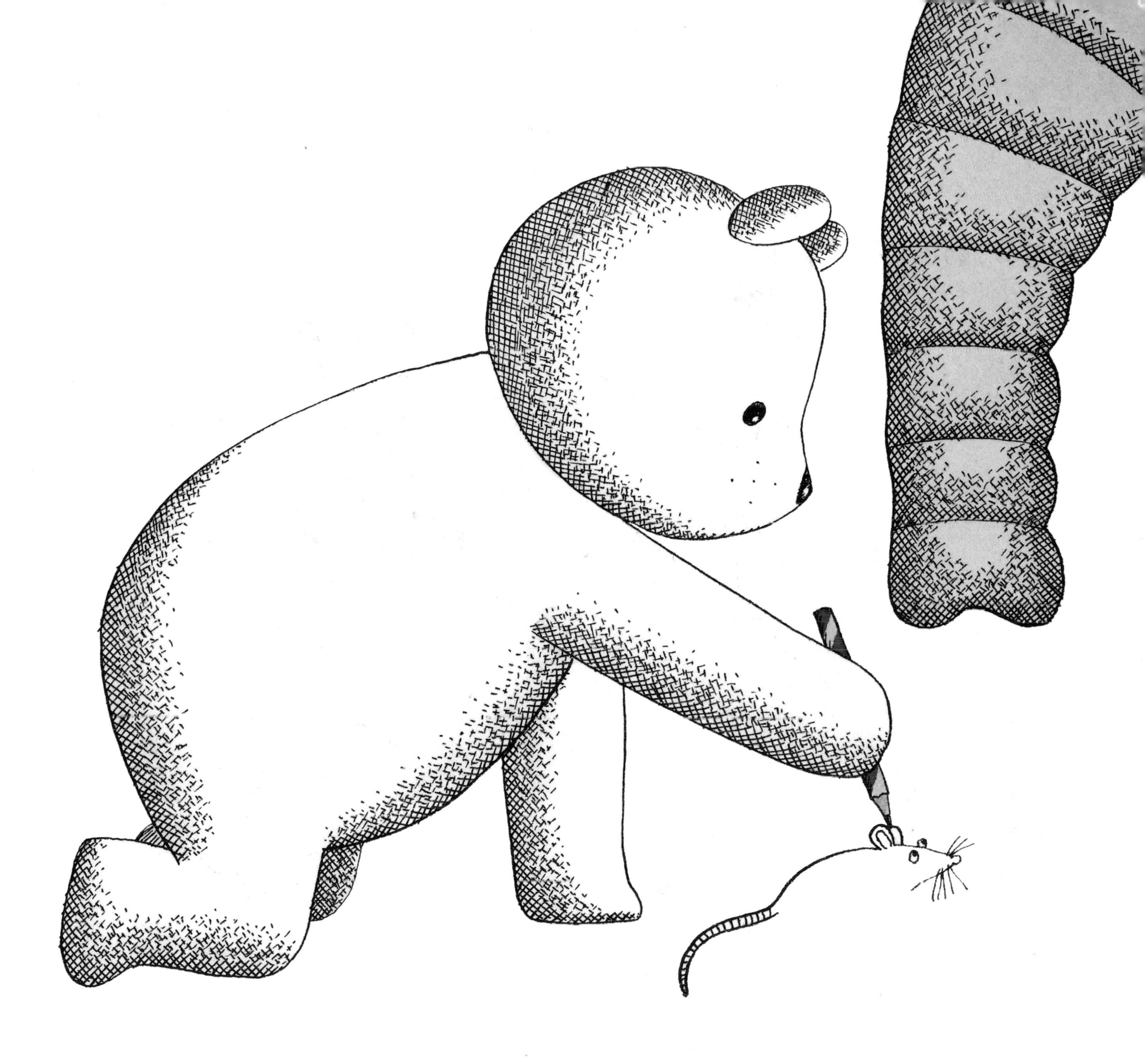

“This will take care of you.”

"Hello, Wall."

“Bye-bye, everyone.”